BLABBER MOUSE

True Kelley

I dreamed I went camping on the moon.

George glued his tail to the table in the art room.

My parents don't know I read under the covers at night.

Joan and Charlotte and I dressed up like scary sharks for Halloween, but everyone thought we were goldfish!

I always do homework at the last minute.

I wrote a poem about peanut butter in mouse fur.

LuLu meowed like a cat, and Mrs. Numley jumped up the wall!

When I play the drums, my whole family wears earplugs.

George laughed and splattered berry juice all over JoJo's glasses!

My crazy nut weirdo sister has a pierced tail.

I promised not to tell... so can you guess how old my dad is?

Today school lunch tasted like cat food.

Dutton Children's Books • **New York**

This book is for Charlotte and Eloise Lindblom

...but it's about ME !

Thanks to Donna Brooks and Debbie Cantrell

Copyright © 2001 by True Kelley
All rights reserved.

CIP Data is available.

Published in the United States by Dutton Children's Books,
a division of Penguin Putnam Books for Young Readers
345 Hudson Street, New York, New York 10014
www.penguinputnam.com
Designed by Richard Amari
Printed in Hong Kong · First Edition
2 4 6 8 10 9 7 5 3 1
ISBN 0-525-46742-4

Blabber Mouse liked to talk and talk.

He talked about his friends...

and his hobbies...

and his adventures...

and what he saw

and where he'd been

and things he remembered.

He told stories. He told jokes.

He recited his own poetry.

But, sometimes he also spread gossip, and worst of all, he told secrets—other people's secrets, things his friends trusted him not to tell.

He didn't mean to. Somehow, the words just popped out. Usually Blabber felt terrible about it afterward.

Once, at school, when Blabber was hungry, his friend LuLu gave him a cheesy-chip cookie from her secret supply.

 Blabber told Kate where the cookies were,

and then he told Charlotte,

and then he told JoJo.

They each borrowed just *one* from LuLu's supply. They were not greedy.

The next time LuLu went to get a cheesy-chip cookie, they were all gone. LuLu guessed what had happened.

"You owe me cookies, Blabber," she said. "Big time."

"Why do you fall all over yourself when you walk by LuLu's desk?" Blabber asked JoJo one morning.

"I have a secret crush on her," JoJo whispered. "I just get nervous around her."

Blabber thought that was so sweet…

…he told LuLu.

LuLu was so embarrassed, she hid behind her tail every time JoJo stumbled by.

Another time, Blabber's friend Charlotte told him that her twenty-eight cousins were coming to stay for a week. "Last night my mom was a nervous wreck running around the house!" she said.

"Charlotte's mom wrecked their house last night," Blabber told his friends.

Of course, it turned out she hadn't wrecked anything at all. Blabber's friends realized he was only blabbing again.

"He can't help it," they said. "He just can't keep his big mouth shut."

And Blabber couldn't.

One day at school, George whispered to Blabber, "Mrs. Numley has a tiny tattoo by her armpit, but I can't tell what it is!"

Of course, Blabber just had to tell *somebody*. So he told everybody!

Mrs. Numley thought it was odd that the class suddenly paid so much attention when she wrote on the board.

Sometimes Blabber's blabbing gave away surprises—even his own. When it was his big sister's birthday, he found the perfect present for her—a Ratty Boys poster. He was so excited about it, he had to tell someone what it was. So...

...he told his big sister!

When she opened her present, she was no good at pretending. "What a surprise," she said.

Then there was the time Blabber went with his friends Joan and George to see his favorite scary movie, *Kitties at Play*. He'd seen it sixteen times. The movie opened with a very frightening scene.

"Don't be scared," Blabber told them. "By the end, the kitties all become friends with the mice."

"Blabber!" howled Joan and George. "You ruined the whole movie!"

Not long after that, Mrs. Numley had a bad Friday. She got to school late, wearing her dress inside out.

She had recess duty in a sudden downpour.

Then there were five fire drills.
Before noon, she sat on her sandwich.

After lunch, JoJo was sick in the wastebasket.

By the end of the day, Mrs. Numley stood at the door looking particularly frazzled. "Class dismissed," she said weakly.

"She forgot homework!" George whispered to Blabber.

"Mrs. Numley, you forgot homework!" Blabber called out before he could stop himself.

"Thanks for reminding me," said Mrs. Numley.

That was the last straw! Blabber's friends knew they had to stop him before he blabbed again.

But how?

On Monday, when Blabber got to school, everyone was working busily in the art room.

During recess, they worked busily in the school kitchen.
Blabber couldn't figure out what was going on.
He felt a little left out.

After school, Blabber saw Charlotte and Mrs. Numley coming out of a store downtown. When they saw him, they acted sneaky and scurried off.

The next day, George dragged a big, lumpy package to school and put it in the closet. When Blabber asked what it was, George said, "If I were you, Blabber, I'd probably tell you."

And Joan said, "If I were you, I'd say we were giving you a Kool Kat Battery-Operated Guitar!"

Blabber was surprised.

And LuLu said, "If I were you, Blabber, I'd tell you that Joan has a crush on you."

Now Blabber was embarrassed. And confused.

Later that afternoon, Mrs. Numley sent Blabber to the office to pick up some new chalk.

When Blabber got back, everyone jumped up and yelled, "Surprise!"

The room was decorated with colored paper and balloons. There were plates full of cheesy-chip cookies and pitchers of berry juice. Everybody had on silly party hats, even Mrs. Numley.

Blabber was very surprised. But why are they giving me a party? he wondered. It's not my birthday.

JoJo handed Blabber some juice and cookies. Charlotte gave him a hat. Music came on, and everyone started crazy-dancing. Blabber was too embarrassed to dance with Joan. He felt like hiding behind his tail.

Suddenly the music stopped. George put the big, lumpy package in front of Blabber. Blabber knew what it would be.

Sure enough, it was just what Joan had said—a Kool Kat Battery-Operated Guitar.

"What a nice surprise," Blabber said politely.

"Now you can put your poems to music," explained George. "Your poems are our favorite kind of blabbing."

Then Mrs. Numley handed Blabber a little present wrapped up and tied with a ribbon.

"This is another gift from the whole class," she said.

No one had told Blabber anything about it. They had all kept their big mouths shut!

Blabber thought that was amazing.

Blabber tore off the wrapping. This present was a *real* surprise.

Inside was a little book with a lock and key. On the cover was written: *Blabber Mouse's Top Secret Diary.*

"Now when you know a secret," Mrs. Numley said, "and you feel you just have to tell someone, you can write it down in your diary, lock it up, and keep the secret safe."

For once, Blabber was speechless. Finally he said, "Thank you so much, everyone. I'm lucky to have friends like you."

"Let's dance," shouted George, and he turned on the music.

But Blabber sat down quietly in a corner and unlocked his new little book.

Slowly, he wrote his first secret.

He thought how much fun it would be to tell everyone. But instead, he thought some more and wrote another secret.

He closed his diary and locked it. Now both secrets were safe with Blabber.

He tucked the diary into his backpack.

And then he asked Joan to dance.